Perfectly
POPPY

Snowy Surprise

Written by Michele Jakubowski

Illustrated by Erica-Jane Waters

Raintree is an imprint of Capstone Global Library Limited, a company incorporated in
England and Wales having its registered office at 7 Pilgrim Street, London, EC4V 6LB
– Registered company number: 6695582

www.raintreepublishers.co.uk
myorders@raintreepublishers.co.uk

Text © 2014 by Picture Window Books
First published in the United Kingdom in paperback in 2014
The moral rights of the proprietor have been asserted.

Designers: Heather Kindseth Wutschke, Kristi Carlson and Philippa Jenkins
Editor: Catherine Veitch
Originated by Capstone Global Library Ltd
Printed and bound in China

ISBN 978 1 406 28048 7 (paperback)
18 17 16 15 14
10 9 8 7 6 5 4 3 2 1

British Library Cataloguing in Publication Data
A full catalogue record for this book is available
from the British Library.

Contents

Chapter 1
The inside day

On Saturday morning, Poppy woke up and looked out of the window. She knew it was going to snow, but she didn't know it was going to snow so much!

"I know just what I want to do today," Poppy said.

Poppy hopped down the stairs and into the kitchen.

"Good morning, Poppy," her mum said. "Would you like some porridge with raisins?"

"Yes please," Poppy said.

Poppy's older brother, Nick, jumped up from the table.

"I finished my breakfast," he said. "I'm going outside now."

"Don't forget your hat and gloves!" yelled Poppy's mum as Nick rushed out of the door.

Once she finished her porridge,

Poppy was ready for her perfect day.

Unlike Nick, her perfect day did not

involve going outside in the cold.

Just last week Poppy had slipped

on some ice and hurt her arm. She

did not want that to happen again.

Poppy grabbed her favourite furry blanket. She snuggled on the sofa. Then she switched on the television.

"Don't you look comfy," said Poppy's mum.

"I am!" Poppy said.

Poppy pulled up her blanket.

"Nick's crazy," she said. "Who would want to play outside in the snow and cold?"

Chapter 2

Change of plans

Poppy watched television for a while. But she was soon bored.

"I'm bored," she complained to her mum.

"You can always go outside,"

her mum said.

"No way. I guess I'll just read,"

Poppy said.

After finishing her favourite book,

it was time for lunch. Nick came in

to eat.

"Why are you still in your pyjamas?" he asked. "You should come outside and play. It's fun!"

Nick's cheeks were pink. His nose was bright red. That didn't look like much fun to Poppy.

"No way," Poppy said. "After lunch I'm watching some more television."

"It would be good for you to go outside and play," said Poppy's mum.

"No thanks, Mum," Poppy said.

She got up from the table and headed for the sofa.

"I don't think so," Poppy's mum said. She turned Poppy towards the stairs. "Go and put on some warm clothes. You need to get some fresh air and exercise young lady."

Poppy marched slowly up the stairs. She didn't want to go outside. This was not part of her perfect day.

Poppy took a long time to get dressed. Her mum made her put on a hat, gloves and a scarf.

When she went outside, Poppy
stood in the snow with her arms
folded. Her mum made her go outside.
She couldn't make her have fun.

Chapter 3
The snowball fight

After a few minutes of sulking,

Poppy felt a snowball hit her back.

Poppy didn't like playing in the

snow, and she really didn't like being

hit with a snowball!

"Got you!" Nick shouted. He was making another snowball to throw.

Poppy scooped up some snow and made a snowball. She quickly threw it. The snowball hit Nick on the arm.

Nick looked surprised. "Wow, Poppy! Nice shot! You can be on my team."

"Team? Who else is out here?"
Poppy asked.

"Everyone!" Nick said.

"You should have said something! You know I hate to miss out on fun things," Poppy said.

"Now you know. Let's get busy," Nick said.

Poppy followed Nick behind a big tree. They made a huge pile of snowballs. Then they made a plan. Poppy was getting excited.

"I'll run out first," Nick said. "You follow me and hit the others with snowballs."

"We can call our plan 'the snowy surprise'," Poppy said.

"Great! Ready?" Nick asked.

"Yes!" Poppy shouted.

Nick and Poppy made a great team. Poppy was good at throwing. Nick was very fast. Together they dodged snowballs and got the other teams.

After a while the other children

had to go home.

"Do you want to go inside?"

Nick asked.

"Not yet," Poppy said.

Nick smiled. "Shall we make
a snowman?"

"I've got a better idea!" Poppy
said. "Let's make a giant trophy
out of snow. After all, we were the
winners of the snowball fight."

And even though it was cold outside, Poppy had a warm feeling inside.

"Now THIS is the perfect day," Poppy said with a smile as she started to make their snow trophy.

"You're right about that," Nick said.

0 0 0 0 0 9 9 9

2 2

9 9 9 9 9 9

7

Poppy's new words

I learned so many new words today! I wrote them down so that I could use them again.

complain say you are unhappy about something

dodge avoid something by moving quickly

involve include something as a necessary part

snuggle curl up and get warm

sulk push out your lip when you are angry or disappointed

trophy prize such as a cup or a medal for winning a competition

Poppy's thoughts

After my day in the snow, I had some time to think. Here are some of my questions and thoughts from the day.

1. Do you like to play inside or outside? Why?

2. Watching television is fun, but why is it important to go outside and play?

3. I didn't want to go outside, but once I did, I had a lot of fun. Write about a time when you did something you didn't want to do.

4. Nick and I did lots of fun things in the snow. Talk about your favourite thing to do in the snow.

Cold day menu

When it's cold outside, I like a lot of warm food to fill my tummy. Here are my favourite meals for cold days.

Breakfast:

Porridge with raisins and milk

Lunch:

Chicken soup, a toasted cheese sandwich, an apple, and milk

Snack:

Hot chocolate with banana bread

Dinner:

Lasagna with garlic bread, a salad and milk

Make a menu of your favourite cold day foods. Then help your mum or dad with the shopping and make the meals. Yum!

Snow day fun

Once I went outside, I found lots of fun things to do in the snow. Here is a list of snow activities for you. Dress warm and try something new!

- build a snowman or an entire snow family

- make a snow angel

- help clear snow from the paths

- throw snowballs

- make a snow castle (instead of a sandcastle)

- go sledging

About the author

Michele Jakubowski grew up in Chicago, United States of America (USA). She has the teachers in her life to thank for her love of reading and writing. While writing has always been a passion for Michele, she believes it is the books she has read over the years, and the teachers who introduced them, that have made her the storyteller she is today. Michele lives in Ohio, USA, with her husband, John, and their children, Jack and Mia.

About the illustrator

Erica-Jane Waters grew up in the beautiful Northern Irish countryside, where her imagination was ignited by the local folklore and fairy tales. She now lives in Oxfordshire with her young family. Erica writes and illustrates children's books and creates art for magazines, greeting cards and various other projects.